After the

Final

Curtain

Social Sinners 5

TL Travis

Sapphire Publishing

COPYRIGHT

Dedication:
To my readers and Social Sinners fans,
Without you, book five wouldn't be here, which means neither would I. Thank you for pushing me to succeed and always do my best.
Until we meet again, I'm sending all my love to you and your family.
~TL

THE FOLLOWING SONGS IN THIS BOOK WERE WRITTEN AND COPYRIGHTED BY TL TRAVIS:

Blood Brothers
Black
Time to Move On
Don't Doubt Us
Who I've Become
You Were Always There
A Heart Divided
Cheap Vodka
The Curtains of My Heart

Northlane - Bloodline
Killswitch Engage - Unleashed
Iron Maiden – The Trooper
Marilyn Manson – The Beautiful People
Metallica - Battery
Pantera – This Love
Black Sabbath – Heaven and Hell
Seether – Fine Again
Five Finger Death Punch – Wrong Side of Heaven
Metallica – Seek & Destroy
Flyleaf – Fully Alive

CONTENTS

CHAPTER ONE

Joey

"That was one hell of a way to end a performance on a high note!" Sal cheerily announced as we exited the stage at the awards show, his smile as wide as the moon. "Welcome to the family son," he told Diamond before pulling him into a hug.

Since coming out, our stoic drummer had finally found his happy place. Well, between that and re-connecting with his mother and brother, he'd become a whole new man. Don't get me wrong, he was still the Social Sinners class clown, but now his humor wasn't used to mask the pain I knew was lurking beneath it. Instead, it was sincere happiness rising to the surface. Nothing made me happier than to see this side of him.

I can't deny the reluctance I felt when he first reconnected with his brother and later his mother. The fear was always there that they'd be no better than his piece of shit father, but thankfully they proved me wrong.

When Easton approached us with his idea on how to propose and shared Diamond's fumbled attempt while he was in rehab, well, there wasn't a snowball's chance in hell we weren't gonna help him out with this. Not to mention the fact that the song Diamond had written for him was by far the best one he'd penned to date, and Stoli and I were excited to perform it. In all actuality, I'd say it was in my top five favorites from the Social Sinners song library. Diamond hadn't pitched it to the team yet, but I think after tonight's performance, he'll be open to letting us write the music and produce it for our next CD. Man, who new Diamond had a poet trapped beneath that gruff exterior?

My brothers and I had come a long way since we first met our freshman year of high school. Through the pain of family drama, loss, attempted suicide, and addiction, our bond never faltered. We made a thousand and one mistakes while walking the paths we'd traveled yet here we were, ready to embark upon our first European tour with our friends who'd long since become an extended part of our family—Maiden Voyage. Man, the way they came through for us time and again just blew me away. Never once did they ask for anything in return. No hidden agenda or devious subplot was behind each thoughtful gift they extended our way. They were just all-around great guys with huge fucking hearts.

Pictures taken of the four of us over the years adorned the walls of our home office. My favorites were the ones of us standing at the front of the stage after performing for the first time at our high school talent show. Our arms were proudly swung around each other's shoulders as we took a bow. Pride radiated through our massive smiles. Right beside that one was the same pose taken a few years later after performing at our first sold-out show. On the desk beside the frame that held a picture of Stoli and me on our wedding day sat the photo Easton had snapped of our band when we signed our first contract, the one with Masterson Management.

Now here we were, headliners, hitting the road on their first tour outside of US soil. Embrace the

Fear was the band Sal had chosen as our opening act. They're way green behind the ears, but I think they'll do alright. They'll fuck up just like we did, but it's how they choose to fix those mistakes that will shape them into the men they'll become. It'll be kinda fun to watch them grow, plus the fact that they were already scared shitless of Diamond that would help keep them in line.

I remember our first tour, living out of a van and scraping together every penny we could to grab shitty hotel rooms here and there. Showering at venues, sleeping in rest stops and doing our best to not succumb to the drug and alcohol scene of life on the road as many had.

Me, well I guess I did falter to some extent after my failed relationship, but when that threatened to get me kicked out of the band, I somehow managed to pull my head out of my ass and straighten up. For some, that never happens, which is sad. You don't just wake up one day and say you want to be in a band and bam, you're in and storming the charts. It's something you must work hard at and pimp yourself like mad. It's the dream of every twelve-year-old with a guitar. To have it all come to an end because of bad decisions is a waste of time and talent, in my opinion.

To this day we will stop and sign autographs for as many fans, especially kids, as we can. Seeing their smiling faces reminds me of Stoli and me when we were their age. Music was and always will be a huge part of our lives. Lyrics that resonated deeply, guiding us through the uncertainty of our adolescence when the four of us were those outcasts that our peers discarded. Yet, here we stood, coming off stage at the Billboard Music Awards to the announcement that our new CD that had released this very morning had already climbed its way up the charts on its debut day. We'd become those who we'd idolized, still idolized to be quite honest, which was something we'll never take for granted. Without our fans, our families and our management team, we'd still be virtual nobody's.

Backstage was packed after the show, filled with the proud faces of our family, which had more than doubled over the last few years. I now had a stepmom, Maggie. She'd been more of a mother to me than the woman who gave birth to me had. My stepbrother, Brad, and his boyfriend, Jackson, had become the friends Stoli and I hung out with as often as we could. Then there was Brandon, Stoli's little brother, who got us through many dark days. Without Brent's help, every step of the way things would've gone south more times than I could count. The support of Mickey's parents David and Beth, his younger sister Julia— as well as his significant others Benny and River– jumping in when we needed them, was beyond awesome. His mom's care packages filled to the brim with home-baked goodies carried us through many a road performance. River was now overseeing the bands website and social media accounts since managing the band had become more than a fulltime job for Easton. There aren't enough words to cover what Easton and Sal have done for us. To know that Easton was going to be a permanent fixture in the family brought the band full circle. And now with the addition of Diamond's mom Sharon and his brother Jay, our support system was entirely in place.

In my reverie, eyeing my band brothers in turn, my wandering eyes find Stoli's gorgeous face staring back at me. To this day, his smile still makes me weak in the knees. And when he winks at me from across the room as he just did, the butterflies it evokes wreaks havoc on my guts—but in the best of ways. The first word to pop into my head every time I see him is, *home*.

Here we are, backstage at the MGM Grand Resort in the middle of the Las Vegas strip, hob-knobbing with those who we've idolized forever. If someone tried to wipe the grins from our faces, it would be wasted efforts on their part. Champagne flutes were being passed around on trays by the wait staff. A lavish buffet was set up along the sides adorning the pathway in an extensive line of linen-draped tables. Alcohol freely flowed, poured by the hands of the hired bartenders strategically located throughout the venue. There were talks of collaborations amongst old friends. Idols and fans connected as new friends, acquaintances reconnected, and then there was me– fanboying off to the side. Totally in awe of the celebrity status flanking the aisles and having the best fucking time of my life.

I can't deny the unease that occasionally crept up inside me in such an elite setting, making me feel like I didn't belong. The lonely broke-ass kid from Everett, Washington, growing up on ghetto ass sandwiches purchased with our monthly food stamp stipend. The embarrassment my father felt at having to accept such help. As a child, I never noticed the pain and anguish he felt in having done so but reflecting back, I can see it clear as day. And still, here we were, the tables have long since turned, and I'm the one who's able to help. It took a lot of convincing, but the warmth that filled me when my dad finally agreed to let me pay off his mortgage with my first big royalty check gave me a sense of worth — being able to pay it forward to the man who'd worked so hard to keep us afloat all those years. Stoli's mom stepping in and acting as my surrogate, even while my birth mother was around, allowed my father to be able to work the extra hours he needed to, and she made sure I was taken care of. Even thinking about it now caused me to tear up. How selfless Stoli's family was to us, and all these wonderful people who entered our lives and never left — always treating us like...*family.*

"Joey?" I looked up at the sound of my name being called, stunned to find the voice belonged to fucking Jonathan Davis! *It's fucking Jonathan Davis!!!* My inner child danced, my heart raced, and suddenly I couldn't breathe. I know he sees the emotional turmoil I'm battling written all over my face as he smiles knowingly back at me.

"Deep breath dude, I'm a huge fan," he says reassuringly, extending his hand for which I did nothing more than stare at blankly.

"Um, what?" *What an idiot, that's all you can say to your idol?* I feel Stoli's hand on my back, tracing calming circles with his fingertips, shaking me from this ridiculous fan-boy mode I'd allowed myself to get sucked into.

"Stoli," he covers for me, stretching his hand out to the rock God himself, "nice to meet you, Jonathan."

"I love your lyrics, wouldn't mind kicking out a couple with you guys. Sal manages your band, right?" he asks, looking back and forth between the two of us. But I'm still unable to find my words.

"Actually, I do. I'm Easton Masterson. Sal's son," Easton said as he walked up behind him. They exchange pleasantries as I stand here staring like an open-mouthed baboon wondering how East stays so calm, cool and collected in the face of music royalty.

"Ah, the mastermind behind the elegant proposal?" Jonathan joked, shaking his hand in return. "Nicely done."

"I thought so," Diamond added, kissing Easton's cheek before shaking Jonathan's hand.

"Babe," Stoli whispers in my ear, "breathe," he reiterated Jonathan's earlier words as he resumed the soothing strokes along my spine.

"Jonathan Davis," I blurted out, louder than I should've as is par for me. I definitely missed the *Whispering 101* class growing up. Unfortunately, my words were loud enough that the man himself heard and glanced over, quizzically before forcing an uneasy grin. *I am such an idiot.* My one chance to meet the singer I idolized most, and I more than blew it. W*ay to make a lasting impression, jackass.*

"Come on," Stoli nudged me with his shoulder. We walked over to where Easton and Jonathan stood, "Jonathan, sorry about that. Joey here has worshipped you since we were kids and he got a bit tongue-tied when you walked up."

"Um yeah," I said, holding a shaky hand out, feeling like a total fool, "sorry about that, I'm Joey."

He laughed, "Yeah, I got that much. I was just filling Easton in on some ideas I'd like to kick around with you guys. I think we could come up with some seriously tight lyrics between us. What do you think?"

"What do I think?" I sorta yelled, again...and he flinched. Stoli laughed from beside me.

"I swear Jonathan, Joey is not the psycho he's portraying himself to be right now. We'll get Easton to set up a meeting and restrain Joey in the meantime." Thank fuck for Stoli, he handled my less-than-smooth move like a pro. Jonathan thanked him before rejoining his crew.

"Joey, you've gotta get that shit under wraps before we meet with him. I get that you're seeing Korn shaped stars right now, but you need to realize you're not the goofy boy with the band posters all over his bedroom walls anymore. We are in the same league that they are," he said, gesturing to the crowd surrounding us.

"Thank you," I said with a kiss before he walked off to talk to Easton and Diamond.

Feeling like a wallflower once again, which was probably in my best interest right now, I resumed scanning the room for familiar faces to chat it up with. Ryder and Derek were off to the side. Derek was shaking his head, and Ryder was staring off in the direction of Stoli and Diamond. I walked towards them, needing to check-in and make sure everything was alright.

CHAPTER TWO

Ryder

"You've got to stop staring at him like that. Your mouth is hanging open, and you're drooling. You look like a love-struck idiot," Derek's whining voice warned me, not for the first time I might add. But little did he know, it wasn't Stoli who was commandeering my attention this time. Instead, I eyed that glorious man standing protectively nearby. As usual, Derek wasn't about to shut the fuck up and leave well enough alone. I did my best to tune him out, ogling that piece of candy hired to protect our bands for not only tonight but for the upcoming tour we were leaving on in a few weeks. *Social Sinners* and *Maiden Voyage*, hopping across the ocean with *Embrace the Fear* opening for us. This European tour was going to be epic if only Derek would shut the fuck up.

He rambled on and on, grating on my last nerve. "Joey's gonna catch you eye-fucking his man, and then all hell is gonna break loose. They're our friends, and we do *not* need that drama out on the road with us."

"What the fuck did you just say?"

Derek and I turned, finding Joey standing behind us.

"Fuck," Derek muttered, rubbing his hand over his jaw.

"You have no one to blame for this but yourself. Just couldn't keep your fucking mouth shut, could you? You're fixing this mess, and by the way, that wasn't who I was staring at," I stalked off, heading toward the dressing room and leaving Derek to deal with Joey.

Stoli and I were a thing of the past, long before he and Joey ever even hooked up. I can't deny he'll always have a piece of my heart, but he was honest with me from the get-go– it was nothing more than a hook-up. Wasn't his fault my heart didn't get that message. I'll never forget the look on his face the day I uttered those three little words, and his face paled. He broke it off right then and there, and that damn near did me in. I sunk so deep inside myself that I scared not only myself but every member of my band. Ironically, some of our best lyrics came from the darkness I'd succumb to. I'm just glad no one ever knew how close I came to ending it all.

Stomping off, much as I imagined a two-year-old would do, the heaviness of my steel-toed boots echoed down the corridor along with another's. I wasn't in the mood to deal with Derek, and he knew he fucked up big time. Entering the dressing room, I slammed the door behind me, hoping he'd take the hint and leave me the fuck alone. But I wasn't so lucky. *Well, time to have it out once and for all.*

"Why can't you take a hint?" I asked as I spun around, surprised to find it wasn't Derek who was standing there.

"Care to explain to me what *that* was all about? You have some sick fetish with my husband?" Joey stood, arms crossed, jaw clenched and looking beyond pissed.

"Look, contrary to what you just heard, I'm more than over Stoli. Besides, that wasn't who I was watching anyway," I told him. I know this wasn't

Joey's fault, but between his defensive stance and the adrenaline pumping through my veins, I feared I was about to go head to head with someone I considered a friend. *Deep breath Ryder. In, one, two, three. Out, one, two, three, repeat.* When I opened my eyes, there stood the man in question, rendering me speechless.

"Hey, I'm talking to you!" Joey yelled. Obviously, I had a problem focusing when Mr. Tall, dark and stoic stood nearby. He eyed me curiously, raising a brow but making no move until Joey shoved me.

"What the fuck Joey?" I cursed, ready to push him back when G.I. Joe jumped between us. Easily pushing us apart with his massive arm span.

"Joey, stop!" Stoli hollered as he barreled into the room. "Ryder and I hooked up long before you and I were even a thing."

"Oh yeah, then why the fuck is he still eyeing you like a piece of candy?"

Joey was usually pretty mellow, seeing him this riled up was new to me. "Dude, for the last fucking time. I wasn't eyeing your man!" I was quickly reaching my breaking point, which was not a good place for me to be in– for myself, or anyone else who was around when I blew. The media would have a fucking heyday and spew all kinds of nonsense about two battling bands hitting the road together. I'd had my anger under control for a long time and setting that beast loose again would reopen old wounds I didn't care to have festering. *Leave the past in the past Ryder...* Unfortunately, Joey didn't share in my Zen philosophies.

At this point, our dressing room had become a stage of its own, filled with every member of Social Sinners, their spouses, and my Maiden Voyage bandmates.

"I take it Joey found out about you and Stoli," Jaxson's dumbass nonchalantly stated loud enough for all to hear.

Joey turned to Stoli, "Did everybody know but me?"

"Come on, babe, this isn't the time or place for us to have this conversation," Stoli reached for Joey, but he pulled away and stormed out.

"Thanks, guys," Stoli complained before following behind him. Dutifully, Max followed suit, leaving me breathless in his wake.

"Do you have any idea what you just did?" I yelled at Derek, pacing back and forth, which was quite the task considering our room now housed nine full-grown bodies in it.

"Anyone care to tell the rest of us what the hell just happened?" Mickey eyed the two of us, waiting for an answer. "Did Jaxson say something about you and Stoli?"

"Derek's got a big fucking mouth, that's what just happened. Fuck," I muttered, dropping down onto the couch. "Stoli and I used to hook up way, way, wayyy before Joey even looked at him that way. It's been over for a long ass time."

"Oh...whoa," Mickey replied, shocked by my declaration. Diamond and Easton didn't look surprised at all. River and Benny stood there with their mouths hanging open. They probably didn't know that Joey and Stoli hadn't been an item since birth, considering the fact that they'd always been glued together like Siamese twins. Shadow, a man of few words, grabbed a bottle of water from the fridge and camped out in the corner seat to watch the show.

"Come on guys," Easton said, "dad and the others are in the hall waiting for us."

"Fix it!" Diamond said, more like demanded. He was the Social Sinners muscle as Shadow was for us, who stared back at Diamond, daring him to make the next move. I swear you could feel the negative energy fill the room when their eyes met. They'd always gotten along well enough, but I knew both were fiercely loyal to their band brothers and would go to war for us if the need ever arose. I only fucking hoped that day would never come. Thankfully, Diamond left. Slamming the door so hard the hinges squeaked in protest.

I needed to talk to Joey, clear the air but now wasn't the right time. He was too far gone, and it wouldn't go well with either of us, we weren't in the right mindset for it. I was surprised that Stoli had never told him about us. Man, that shit was years ago. *Yeah, and it took me a ridiculous amount of time to get over him, and no matter how many beds I tainted, it didn't help ease the pain.* But seeing them together as a couple just made sense. At first, I have to admit, it was awkward but attending their wedding really put things into perspective for me. Some couples you could tell when you looked at them that they were meant to be together, that was Joey and Stoli. My forever? Well, I'd never thought much past getting off. Although as of late, I had to admit I felt like something was missing. The empty bed at night scenario was getting rather...old. *As was I.*

"Earth to Ryder," Shadow said, thumping me on the head with a drumstick.

"Ouch. Dude, what the fuck?"

"You zoned out. We've been talking to you for like fifteen minutes," Shadow laughed as he beat his sticks on the arm of the black leather couch.

"It hasn't been fifteen minutes. It's only been a couple. Look, I didn't know Joey was standing behind me, or I never would've said anything. It's Stoli's problem to deal with. His dumbass should've said something a long time ago. Either way, you should be over him by now man, let it go, Olaf," Derek said. Making jokes wasn't his forte and ninety-nine percent of the time they were Disney related, which was just creepy as fuck.

"You know, you're really starting to piss me off," I stood far too abruptly forcing everyone else to their feet as well. They probably thought I was gonna haul off and deck Derek and were preparing to pull us apart. Much as I'd like to right now, I knew that wouldn't solve shit, and I'd only regret it later. Pissed or not, he has been my best friend for a long time. "I am over him, and for the millionth time, I wasn't fucking staring at him!"

"Dude, did you see their fucking bodyguard? I'd climb that mountain like a fucking champ," Jaxson exclaimed, quickly diverting my anger in his direction as I released a growl. That mountain, as he called him, was on my radar and if anyone was gonna climb him— it was going to be me.

"Um, I think we now know who he was staring at," Shadow said, stating the obvious.

My band brothers were utterly oblivious to what happened after the show in Memphis between Max Hightower and me. The thought of that man buried so fucking deep inside me I saw stars had me jacking off more times than I could count. The question now was, does he even remember me?

CHAPTER THREE

Max

I had my work cut out for me with taking the new security position watching the guys from *Social Sinners* and *Maiden Voyage* when they hit the road together. And yeah, I'd probably bitten off more than I could chew with this job, but who wouldn't want to chew on the likes of Ryder Hampton? The guy was a force of nature all by himself. The kind of man who crawled under your skin and set up camp, even after the Park Rangers told him to get the fuck out. His face was one of those that bordered other-worldly, with soulful eyes, and long, wild hair that always looked wind-blown or bed messy. I liked the visual of him being in bed, so I was going with bed messy hair instead of the Fabio wind-blown image that wanted to push its way into my head.

Fabio is not my roll. Ryder most definitely is.

I preferred complex, multi-layered men who knew what they wanted and had the balls to de-mand it and take it. I also liked men who had me wanting to unzip my pants from nothing more than a shared, heated gaze that oozed the promise of happy, carnal endings. I needed to be challenged too, and Ryder sure as fuck checked off all my boxes in that regard.

I saw glimpses of another side of Ryder during my hours of watching him from afar. I told myself it was all part of my job, and it was. Mostly. Studying our Principals was how we got to know their habits, and that helped us to protect them better. All in a day's work – or so I had convinced myself. But below the surface, I saw a man who looked like he might need help sorting through his personal baggage. A guy who definitely needed protection but didn't believe he did, and I was confident I was the perfect man to fill all of his job requirements.

When my old boss, Fizzbo offered me a transfer to a new security guard unit to help both bands, I almost turned down the position. I loved the guys I was working with at Ventura Security. But with the lure of a pay increase and more in-field details, it was an offer I couldn't refuse. The other bonus was being able to see Ryder regularly but as sweet as that aspect of the job would be, I needed to be careful about it too. I was hired to protect their asses, not fuck them.

I knew I was in trouble from the first day I saw him, which I'm sure didn't register on Ryder's radar– but my radar? It pinged for hours after we walked in opposite directions and continues to sound alarm bells to this day any time he's close by. I have a unique ability to sense when he's near. I can feel the fine hairs on my body lift, and my skin begins to prickle with heat. Or maybe I'm just seriously horny, and I can smell his pheromones. Whatever it is, when I feel it, I know he's in my orbit.

I had my doubts on whether he remembered my damn name, never mind that we'd been formally introduced by Fizzbo weeks ago. I sensed Ryder's confusion of my identity every time his gaze tripped over me in the hallway. There was always that sud- den *"who the fuck is that"* moment that floated across his eyes then turned into a frustrated glare whenever he saw me. At least that's how it looked to me. I got the feeling my presence with their security team was more annoying than it was intriguing for him. Whatever. I was there to do a job, and I would do it above and beyond my training to keep him and their bands safe. I could jerk-off to visuals of his long hair wrapped around my dick for friction on my own time. No crime in that.

Even having all the intel I had on Ryder, I was in no way prepared for what happened after their show in Memphis. But just like him not remembering my name, I wasn't positive he would recall the event. Something that was life-changing for me was probably routine for him.

My earpiece crackled with my boss's voice. "Get into place by the curtain, stage left," I was ordered. "We're about to move the band back down into the green room."

My back went rigid at hearing the directive, and I quickly inserted myself between people to get to my post. Maiden Voyage was taking their final bow of the night at center stage after another incredible performance to a sold-out crowd. That seemed to be the norm for them, though. Seeing them hit the stage every night and own it the way they did was a dream job for me. But I couldn't enjoy the show for more than a few seconds here and there. It was too dangerous. Allowing the lines to blur between being a guard and a fan got our Principals hurt, and that was a chance we couldn't– and wouldn't take.

On this night the energy from the band was at full velocity when they exited the stage. Depending on the vibe they got from their audiences on any given night was how they gauged the input they gave to each show. If their crowd was digging their set, then they played harder. If the audience was slower to become involved, Maiden dug deeper and played their asses off even more. It usually left them completely spent after the show. They'd exit the stage dripping with sweat and hoarse from the high decibels of singing. Stagehands waited just out of sight from the audience with a towel and a bottle of water for each player to grab on their way off stage; the towel to mop themselves, and the water to soothe their parched throats. Then security would flank them and get them out of the area and downstairs for them to relax. That's where I was that night; waiting in the shadows.

I had eyes on Ryder as he lingered on stage to give the audience one last wave. Typical of him to always take up the rear of their exit but I was ready for him. I watched him grab a towel and a bottle of water as he cleared the curtain, and I was already moving in to take up my position behind him when he suddenly stopped short. His movement was so quick I almost slammed into his backside, then he spun around and got in my face. My training reflexes had me wanting to react proactively, but before I could make a move, Ryder made his.

His mouth slammed against mine like a bolt of lightning searing through the sky from an unseen storm cloud. My feet fused to the floor, and my training flew right the fuck out of my head. All I could do was hold on and hope Ryder left behind a big enough piece of my body for my family to give me a proper military burial. One gloriously, taunting sweep of his tongue plundered my mouth, and then he pushed me away. It happened so fast I wondered if I had imagined it purely because it was a constant fantasy running on an endless loop inside my head, but his teasing laughter jerked me back to reality quick enough.

"I was right," Ryder said with a wolfish grin. "You do taste as good as you look."

I stood there for an awkward moment and watched him walk off in the direction of his band as if he hadn't just seriously fucked with my head. It wasn't until I heard the voice of my boss bark out another command in my earpiece that I forced my feet to move from the spot Ryder had made them take root. I caught up to the band with Ryder still lagging at the back edge of the group, and I pur-posefully averted my eyes from him so that I could do my damn job. Ryder obviously had other ideas about that.

The guards ahead of me had created a barrier to get Maiden Voyage into the green room without disruption, and I was to take the last spot at the doorway. Once the band members were all inside the room, we'd close the doors and let them celebrate the success of the show in private while we blocked the doorway and the hall from anyone wanting access to them.

That's how my team had rehearsed it, but Ryder never liked following orders. He stopped at the doorway and faced me. My body flinched at what he might do to me this time, and my hand was already lifting to give him a push into the room if he hesitated too long in place. Then he leaned in closer, that sexy as hell grin still sensuously tugging at his lips, and he fucking winked at me.

"That blush on your face is my new favorite color," Ryder said, and then he stepped into the room where he disappeared in the center of the gathered crowd as if they'd swallowed him whole.

Yeah, Ryder Hampton was going to give me serious trouble on this tour.

And blue balls.

CHAPTER FOUR

Stoli

Well, fuck...

Joey stormed out of the dressing room, fists clenched, and tore off down the hall and right out the side door of the building. I wasn't too worried since Max was right behind him, but we needed to be alone and heading out into the overpopulated Las Vegas strip wouldn't allow for that. Not to mention, it was stupidly dangerous and hot as fuck outside.

"Joey, wait up!" I yelled, just as the heavy metal security door slammed shut. I was in so much fucking trouble, and I had no one to blame for it but myself. Why had I never told him about Ryder and me? *Because you didn't want things to be uncomfortable. Well dumbass, you surpassed that option and dove face-first into hell!*

When I got to him, he was pacing back and forth in the alleyway with Max standing guard nearby. He nodded knowingly to me as I passed him to get to Joey.

"Joey," I panted, bending over to try and catch my breath. "Will you at least look at me?" I instantly regretted asking that once I saw the hurt reflected in those tear-filled hazel eyes. His gaze typically had a window directly into my soul, but right now it was empty, devoid of the love it usually held for me, replaced with pain. *What have I done?*

"Joey, can we please go up to our room and talk about this?" I pleaded, not wanting anyone lurking nearby to get wind of our dirty laundry being aired and have it wind up plastered all over the weekly wipe magazines.

"I think that's a good idea," Max said without turning around. I appreciated him giving us our privacy.

"A crowd is building at the end of the alleyway with their phones in hand." He said something into his earpiece that I didn't quite hear, my sole focus was on Joey. When the side door opened, another security guard and Easton emerged, and we were swiftly herded back indoors.

Joey walked straight toward the private elevator that went up to our rooms with Max. "Diamond and I are going to stay down here for a while longer and work the crowd," Easton told me.

"I think you have your work cut out for you. Good luck," Diamond said, patting me on the shoulder.

"You have no idea how much my friends," I told them as I walked away, arriving at the same time as the elevator did. Joey spoke not a word to me as we stood in opposite ends of the cab on the ride up. It pained me to have so much distance between us. When the elevator came to a stop, Joey raced out and jogged down the hall, the door slamming behind him echoed through the barren corridor. Max muttered, "good luck," before I entered our suite, finding Joey pacing again, back and forth in front of the bank of windows that overlooked the strip.

"Joey, I'm sorry I didn't tell you. But it was a long time ago, way before you and I ever even kissed," maybe that wasn't the best intro into the conversation, but it was all I had.

"It's not the act itself that bothers me as much as the omission. The fact that everyone knew but me. That fucking hurts like hell," he turned, the tears running down his face ripped my fucking heart out.

"Everyone didn't know, at least I didn't think anyone else outside of Maiden knew. I personally never told anyone," I tried to reassure him.

"No, not even your own husband," he declared through clenched teeth. "Did you love him?"

"No, I didn't. And that's what ultimately ended it."

"What do you mean?"

"The day he said I love you, was the day I called it quits. It was nothing more than hook-ups for me, a way to blow off steam. I was incapable of loving anyone else," I answered honestly, although speaking those words aloud made me feel like an insensitive asshole for having discarded Ryder's feelings as quickly as I had. I was young, and stupid and had already given my heart to Joey without him even knowing it.

"That's pretty fucking cold, especially coming from you," Joey said. "Now I feel like shit for going off on Ryder the way I did. I damn near punched him."

That shocked the hell out of me. Joey had never hit another human in his entire life. He and Mickey were the passive ones in our group. Never in a million years would I have expected this reaction from him but the confrontation I walked in on tonight showed me a different side of my husband. One I didn't care to see again.

"Joey, this is on me– not Ryder. I should've told you a long time ago."

"Yeah, you're right. You have no idea how foolish I felt hearing that third hand. That's not the way a husband wants to hear about his spouse having a past fling with a friend. Maiden has been there for us every step of the way. You had a million fucking opportunities to come clean with me and yet you chose not to. What does that say about you?" he asked. With every word he uttered I sunk lower and lower. How could I ever make this up to him or to Ryder for that matter?

Joey sat and began untying his shoes. As I neared, he held his hand up, "Don't. Just. Don't. I can't handle you right now. Maybe it's best if you go back down to the party." I gasped, cut by his words, but deep down, I knew I deserved everything he was dishing out. At least his sadness had progressed to the anger phase, so the tears had stopped. However, anger towards one another wasn't an emotion we'd shared as a couple. At least it wasn't up until now.

Gripping the door handle, I turned, and told him, "I love you, Joey," before leaving.

"Heading back downstairs?" Max asked as I entered the hallway.

"Um, yeah."

"Give me a minute," he said before speaking to whoever was manning the other end of their wireless communication devices, "Rogue One wishes to return to the party." He turned to me, "is Joey going with you or staying in?"

"I think he's staying in." I didn't elaborate any further even though I knew Max got the message. A few minutes later, the elevator doors opened, and out came another member of their security team. Equally as brawny as Max... must be a prerequisite for their jobs. Max let him know Joey was in the room alone before escorting me back downstairs and leaving the new guy to tend to the door duty.

The first thing I did when I got back to the party was to locate Ryder. I owed him an apology– for multiple reasons. Snagging a bottle of water from the table as I passed, I scanned the crowd in search of him. Spotting the mass of bodies he'd collected around him, I noticed Derek tracking me in my peripheral vision. The look on his face spoke to the level of concern he had over the situation and how he thought this was gonna go down. Midway to my destination, he, Jax and Shadow surrounded me. Not far behind them came Diamond and Easton.

"Guys, I'm only going to apologize. I swear," I said, raising my hands in mock surrender. "I know I owe him more than that, but I gotta start somewhere."

"You bet your sweet ass you do," Jax angrily responded while Shadow glowered at me. Fuck, I had a lot of rebuilding ahead of me with these guys. Tonight had started on such a high note. All it took was one past omission to surface and turn my key relationships to shit.

"Guys I promise, I'm gonna make this right for everyone," I don't know what more I could say. It was Ryder and Joey I owed this promise to – not them, but I could tell they weren't about to back down without it. Not to mention the fact that the tour would be total shit if this didn't get resolved.

"Gonna make what right exactly?" Ryder asked from behind me.

"Hey man, can we go somewhere and talk?" I scanned the eyes boring down on us, "privately?"

"Yeah, sure," Diamond and Shadow released a low growl at Ryder's response, reminding me of wild animals warning their enemies, as I'm sure they intended.

We stepped out onto the patio, finding a some-what private break in the crowd. "Look, Ryder," I began, "I still don't know what happened *exactly* because Joey is hardly talking to me, but it's clear I owe both of you an apology."

"I was staring at someone, and Derek thought it was you and made a comment that Joey overheard. I'm sorry he found out about us the way he did, but what I don't understand is why you never told him."

"I've been running that through my skull since I caught Joey rearing back to deck you in the dressing room tonight. It just never came up, but now I know I should've initiated the conversation and let him know a long time ago. But I owe you an apology that dates way past tonight. When we were seeing each other, I discounted your feelings, and you deserved better than that. And for that, I can't apologize enough. I'm truly sorry, Ryder."

"I won't deny it didn't hurt like hell, baring my soul and saying those infamous last words to you," he smirked, but I could see the pain reflected in his eyes. Pain that *I* had caused, "but it is what it is. You and Joey belong together. It took me a long ass time to accept that, but you do."

"It still didn't give either of us a reason to discount your feelings," Joey said, both Ryder and I flinched having not heard him walk up behind us. "I'm sorry too, Ryder. I overreacted, and that's not my style," Joey told him, extending his hand in a truce. Ryder stared down at it. I held my breath while waiting for one or the other to respond.

"Dude, we're family. Family doesn't shake hands, family's gotta hug," Ryder said to him in his absolutely worst *Tommy Boy* impression before pulling him into his arms. Within moments, the rest of our band members flanked us. I still had my work cut out with Joey in the form of some significant ass-kissing, but this at least gave me hope that we would be able to mend the rift between us.

We stuck around until about two a.m. when the crowd started to thin, mostly mingling apart from each other. As much as it pained me, I knew Joey needed space, so I left him to do his thing. Seeing as it was literally our first fight as a couple and the fact that I'd caused it pissed me off to no end. No one could hate me more than I did right now.

When the guys started bowing out, one by one, we weren't far behind them. I could sense Joey's discomfort being alone with me again as we rode the elevator together. There were several others in the cab with us, which forced us to stand side by side. He was so close, yet so far. I wanted to reach out but feared his rejection. The only person in my life who could break me was Joey.

"Joey please, talk to me. Yell at me. Say something but don't ignore me. I'm begging you," I pleaded with him as soon as the door to our room was secured.

Joey blew out a breath, sat down and pulled his hair behind his ears, so it was out of his face. He was thrilled at how fast it was growing back since the accident, the scars that formed where the staples once were had lessened to small knots. "I don't know what to say. That had to be one of the most, probably right at the top of the list, embarrassing moments... situations? I don't even know what the fuck to call it, but it was humiliating."

Wow, I didn't see that coming, nor did I have a reply. *I fucked up— majorly.*

I stood in the entryway, watching him take off his shoes before heading into the bathroom and closing the door behind him without glancing my way. A few minutes later, I heard the shower water turn on. We never showered apart— ever. *Fuck.* Do I leave him be? Do I risk further injury to my psyche by joining him and groveling? Or do I hit the bar downstairs and get fucking plowed?

As tempting as drinking away this nightmare was, I knew that wasn't the answer. All those years ago, I regretted not going after Joey and telling him how I felt. Essentially, letting him slip through my fingers. A weak act from a confused young mind and one I wasn't willing to repeat. If I had to fight for my man and look like a pussy by doing so, well then, so be it.

Not wanting to waste any more time overthinking, I haphazardly discard my clothing, not caring what happened to it or where it landed. I needed to touch him. My body craved his like my lungs required air. Even the slightest of touches shared between the two of us sated me, carried me through the day. But tonight, there were no exchanges of love, and I felt my life source draining. Joey was the elixir that gave me life.

As stealthily as I could, I slipped inside the bathroom only to be had as the frame supporting the glass door to the shower protested when I opened it. Joey didn't even flinch, just continued to lean forward with the warm water beating against the back of his head. His drenched locks hung over his face, masking him from my view. *Even the elements are working against us.*

Standing behind him, my eyes tracked the water droplets as they cascaded down his naked flesh, making me long to be them. They slid further down his spine, over the curvature of his perfect ass, continuing to the entrance I wished to be buried deep inside of. Then they were falling off and swirling into the drain. My fingertips had a mind of their own, no regard for asking permission before relieving the iridescent drops of their duties. A single touch and the sparks reignited, filling me with a sense of hope and *home.*

"Joey," I whispered. "I never meant to hurt you."

He sighed, "I know, but you still did. I felt like such a fool Stoli." Joey stood abruptly, forcing my fingers to slip away.

"Baby, please, tell me how I can make this right?" begging wasn't beneath me, not when it came to the man who owned my heart.

"I just don't know."

"I can't erase the past, if I could, I'd do it in a heartbeat," and I meant every word I said.

"That's something I struggle with myself. But our pasts are what essentially brought us together. I'm not dumb. I knew you slept with others before me. I just never expected it to be Ryder of all people. Are there any other friends of ours you've slept with that I need to be warned about?" he asked, turning to face me for the first time since we entered the suite, and making eye contact. I'm sure he was seeking the truth in my answer and knew without a doubt he'd find it in my eyes.

I held his gaze, I had nothing to hide, not anymore. "No, no one else that you know. At least not that I'm aware of and we pretty much share the same group of friends."

He nodded in acknowledgment, knowing I spoke the truth before his head dropped again, breaking our gaze. I desperately needed to bring him back to me. "Joey," I whispered, cupping his cheeks with my hands and turning his head upward, "I love you."

A single tear fell from his eye, its descent halted by my lips before meeting his. It hadn't been that long since we'd last kissed, yet it felt like forever. I pulled him against me, chest to chest. His arms snaked around my waist while our tongues dominantly dueled. No matter how hard I tried, I couldn't get close enough to him even though every inch of our skin was touching.

"The water's starting to cool, can we move this to the bed?" I eagerly asked.

He spoke not a word. Instead, he chose to nod in response. Hastily we finished showering, barely toweling off before our bodies met beneath the sheets. I was the first to make a move but his reluctance to do so concerned me. I didn't want to jump right into this, married or not if he wasn't in the mood this wasn't going to happen. No means no, and I'd never force him to do something he didn't want to do.

Reaching over, I tucked a stray lock of hair behind his ear, rubbing the pad of my thumb along his jawline as my lips touched his forehead. When that was met with no resistance, I trailed them along the side of his face, nipping his earlobe before my lips descended upon his again. The magnetic pull between us was undeniable. It was like a raging inferno every time we touched.

I slid my hands down, firmly gripping his cheeks, pulling him to me, forcing our erections to grind together. The friction was painfully sweet, the perfect mixture. *Holy hell, I could come so easily from this.* But not tonight. Make-up sex was meant to be more, frotting like horny teens was not the way one says I'm sorry.

My finger traced the outline of his crack, slowly making its way south, the pad massaging the sensitive nerves at his entrance. When the tip breached the outer rim, he released a salacious moan, and my cock bobbed in response.

"Please, Joey, I need to be inside you. I need to feel that connection. Please say yes," I begged.

Breathlessly, he panted the single word I was hoping he'd say, "Yes."

When I leaned over him to retrieve the lube from the nightstand, he began stroking my cock, causing me to pause and enjoy the moment. With each tug, his fingers tightened around my shaft. Slowly, he pulled me toward his mouth and wrapped those beautiful, kiss swollen lips around the head. His tongue swirled around the rim, dipping into the slit while his hand continued its ministrations. My balls were drawing up, and it took all I had to stop this before I came.

"Not like this babe, I need to be inside you," I said before kissing him and returning to my place alongside him.

Reluctantly, I left his lips, trailing a line down his torso with mine, taking each nipple in turn before dipping my tongue into his navel. The sound of the tube lid opening echoed through the quiet room as I squirted some on two fingers, rubbing them together to warm the gel. He spread his legs for me as I drew his cock inside my mouth while my fingers circled his hole. One by one they breached the tight entry, stretching his channel. Watching my fingers slide in and out of him was just as much of a turn on for me as it was to him. When I grazed the spongy surface I sought, he again moaned, arching his back and spread his legs wider.

"Stoli," he murmured, and I knew he was ready for me. Generously, I coated my cock and took my place between his legs, and he drew his knees back. Slowly I pushed in, stilling once I was fully seated inside and released the breath I'd unknowingly held. *Right where I belong.*

"Open your eyes baby," I said to him. When those hazel beauties I'd fallen so hard for found mine, I smiled down at him, "hi."

He grinned, something I feared I'd not see again, "Hello," he replied, lighting up the darkroom with his smile. His hands wound around the back of my neck, pulling me down for a kiss as I began to move inside him. With every shift of my hips, I pegged his spot, clenching my teeth to keep from coming before he did.

"Harder," he moaned, and I obliged. But with every thrust, it became increasingly more difficult to stave off the orgasm that was ready to escape.

"Joey," I pleaded, hoping he'd get the point.

"Almost there."

"Can't...hold on..." I ground out.

"Stoli!" he yelled as I felt his muscles contract around me.

That was all it took as I called out, "Joey!" and came. When the aftershocks had passed, I stared down at the man I loved more than life itself. Sweaty strands of hair stuck to his forehead, yet he'd never looked more handsome to me than he did right then. After I cleaned us up, I laid back down beside him. I pulled his back against my chest as we fell asleep watching the sunrise through the tinted wall of windows in our suite.

CHAPTER FIVE

Mickey and the twins

The two-hour flight back to Seattle was mildly uneventful. I was happy Joey and Stoli made up, or this would've been one uncomfortable ride home. When it came to our previous conquests, River, Benny and I had a *leave the past in the past* rule we lived by. After all, it wasn't like anyone was going to have any random kids popping out of the woodwork. Plus, we'd all been tested a long time ago and were negative. There wasn't anything left to worry about from that aspect either. But I guess the lesson learned from this situation was, keep your mouth shut when you're in a public setting, *Derek*.

With everyone around us getting hitched, I wondered if the fact that we could never legally be married bothered River or Benny. Since both technically worked for the band, they were under the same insurance plan as the rest of us and the company absorbed their premiums, so insurance coverage wasn't a concern. I knew other couples who had to get married just to have affordable coverage. Neither of them said anything about our inability to legalize our relationship, and they were genuinely happy for Diamond and Easton. Still, I couldn't help but wonder if they had any regrets.

"Hey guys," we'd just sat down to dinner. Benny insisted on making homemade lasagna which took him the better part of the day, and he refused to let either one of us help him with it. I leaned over and kissed him before taking my seat at the head of the table. "This looks and smells fantastic, Benny." He smiled lovingly back at me. River had already shoveled a massive bite into his cavern.

The clanking of forks against the porcelain plates filled the room while Benny's culinary expertise delighted our senses. This man never ceased to amaze me, and this lasagna was by far the best I'd ever had. "Benny, this is amazing."

"Why thank you, sir," he flirted, batting his eyelashes at me.

"Agreed, good job man," River added.

"So," I began, uncertain how this was gonna go. What would I do if they were disappointed? Making sure they were happy and that their needs are met, was my first thought with everything I did.

"What's up, Mick?" River asked, goading me after I'd paused for too long.

"Well, with everyone in our circle getting married, I was ah... I was wondering if it bothered you guys that we couldn't legally do it?" There, I said it. Now I'd hold my breath and wait. They both seemed happy all the time, granted our downtime was minimal, but neither of them complained about our busy lives.

"I didn't realize a marriage proposal was on the table?" Benny asked, "did I miss some previous conversation we had?"

"No, I just don't want you guys to have any regrets about being with me. When it was just the two of you, the option was there. But now..." I trailed off, not wanting to finish that thought.

"We could have a commitment ceremony," River quickly added.

"That's true," Benny agreed.

"I'm afraid that if something were to happen to me that you guys would somehow get screwed via the legal system," mental note to self, talk to the band's lawyer and make sure that didn't happen.

"You could always legally marry one of us, and then we could do the commitment ceremony for the triad. I hate the thought of anything happening to you, but you know if something did, that Benny and I would take care of each other. The same goes for you if one of us outlives the other," River added. Morose as it was, it was a potential reality.

"This is depressing as fuck," I said, exasperated. The thought of losing either one of my guys wasn't something I ever wanted to survive. We worked effortlessly as a threesome, and I couldn't see us as a twosome, nor did I want to. "How would I ever be able to choose one of you over the other? I love you both equally."

"It's not choosing," River pointed out, "we'd be committed as a trio, it would only be on paper for those who needed it to be. It's stupid that it has to be that way, but it is what it is. Look, I'll make it easy for you. Go down to the courthouse and marry Benny, then the three of us can hold a commitment ceremony with our friends and family here in the backyard this summer. Deal?"

Wow, River seemed to have fewer qualms with the whole scenario then I did. Maybe I was over-thinking it, but I never wanted them to think I played favorites at any time. "Benny, is that something you'd want to do? You've not said much throughout this entire conversation?"

"Well," he said, shifting in his seat, "this is an unconventional proposal for sure."

"Yeah, for an unconventional relationship," I added.

"True. Are you one hundred percent sure you're okay with this River?" Benny asked him.

"It seriously makes no difference to me Benny. The commitment ceremony matters more than a piece of paper mandated by the government," River assured him.

"Then if these are the proposals you two are offering me, I say…Yes!" He yelled, grinning from ear to ear. Looks like the conversation went better than I'd anticipated. It got a little morbid in the middle, but in the end, we came to an agreement, and I guess we were engaged.

Whoa…I'm engaged…

"I'll call the band lawyer in the morning and get the ball rolling. I want to make sure everything is in both of your names with Benny as the executor since he'll be the legal spouse. Benny, pick a day you want to do this. I'm assuming River will be one of our best men?"

"I'll be Benny's since I'm sure you want Diamond to be yours," River replied, knowing I'd want my best friend to be there.

"Shit, I hope Diamond doesn't think we're over-shadowing their engagement. I need to talk to him first," I said, having realized this decision was in the wake of theirs.

"Just let us know," River said. Benny was bopping around, picking up the dishes while dancing to the beat in his head that he could only hear. That little shit was so damn cute. He was the glue in this re-lationship, although River had strengths he brought to our happy triad as well.

"Well," Benny began as he flittered back into the room and plopped down on my lap.

"Umph," my lungs expelled at the added weight forcing the air from my body.

"Oops, sorry. I think this decision calls for a cel-ebration," he finished.

"What did you have spinning around in that de-vious little mind of yours?" River inquired.

"Well, if memory serves me correctly, I believe we have some unused edible body paints somewhere in this McMansion," Benny reminded us.

River and I eyed one another daringly, the im-pending challenge clearly written across both our faces. But who would make the first move? No sooner had I finished that thought when he bolted upright, knocking his chair backward. I tossed Ben-ny over my shoulder, and we both made a break for the stairs at the same time, and the chase was on, with Benny's laughter echoing through the house.

I tossed a still giggling Benny onto the bed and made a dive for our toy chest at the same time as River. Our housekeeper was not going to be happy when she changed our linens next, but that was the least of my concern, and I paid her well. Right now, my focus was on sating my fiancés insatiable appetites. *Fiancés...* When I turned around, both were staring at me expectantly. Naked and sitting on top of the bed, erections in hand, slowly stroking them. *Fuck me, that's hot.* I'd never get enough of seeing that, knowing those two gorgeous men wanted me. Loved me and had now agreed to spend the rest of their lives with me.

"Is this a party for two, or three?" River asked me, "because one of us is overdressed if it's for three."

I tossed the package his way. He caught it midair while I hurriedly undressed, catching my foot in my pant leg and falling on my ass— much to their enjoyment.

"Shut it," I hollered, laughing at my lack of game. I stayed on the floor to safely finish the task at hand, not wanting to break anything that would serve me well tonight before joining my guys in bed. River passed out two paint dispensers to each of us as I asked, "Now, who gets my autograph on their ass first?" Both turned, looking over their shoulders while wiggling their moneymakers at me. I smacked and nipped each cheek before drawing a heart on Benny's left globe and proceeded to lick the blue raspberry memory away before doing the same to River.

River joined me in turning Benny's body into a work of art, painting his own Rembrandt on Benny's back. The scent of our mischief filled the air, lemon and strawberry were River's flavors of choice. I continued to color our gorgeous canvas with the raspberry and orange I was handed. We licked them away as swiftly as we'd left them, purposely placing them in the areas we wished for our mouths to torment. The tip of the applicator teased the over-stimulated nerves at his entrance as my tongue spread the gelled delight I'd dotted him with, eliciting the most sinful moans in the process.

"Here, let's flip him over," River suggested. Once he was on his back, River traced the vein trailing up his shaft, outlining it in strawberry as his tongue licked it clean, wiping away the fruity remnants. Benny's body was a kaleidoscope of colors, a rainbow of delight. When River reached the tip, I spread Benny's legs apart, my tongue dove in, lapping at his entrance as River orally pleasured him. Benny's incoherent responses filled our ears. Our mouths pleasured him until he screamed. His orgasm hit hard and fast from fucking River's mouth while my tongue did the same to his ass. We continued our ministrations, riding the aftershocks with him.

River crawled up Benny's torso, swiping his tongue across his lips, allowing Benny to get a taste of himself. That act alone had my cock throbbing in response. The taste of one's self from a lover's mouth was like an aphrodisiac. At least in my eyes, it was, and I knew they both felt the same way. *How was I lucky enough to find not only one man but two who enjoyed the same things as I did?*

"I want to feel both of you inside me, at the same time," Benny surprised us with his words. He'd taken each of us in turn before, but this wasn't something we'd attempted yet. And I wasn't quite sure how it would work out. "Please?" he pleaded, that little face was one I wasn't able to say no to. But I couldn't deny that his request was something I'd wanted to try for quite some time now.

"Benny, baby," River trailed off, seemingly as concerned as I was.

"I know," Benny replied, softly kissing him, "I promise to let you both know if it's too much."

"How do you propose we do this exactly?" I asked him, walking through the semantics in my head.

"I'll ride River. Once he's in all the way, I'll lean forward so you can work your way in from behind me."

I nodded in response, chewing on the inside of my mouth as I did whenever I felt nervous or unsure. This concerned me a great deal, Benny was a small man, and while we weren't packing porn star sized meat, it was still a lot for any one body to allow in. But I trusted Benny to know his limits and he said he'd tell us if it was too much.

"Grab the lube," he told me, nodding toward the bottle we kept on the nightstand as he assumed the position hovering above River. "Prep me," he winked and wiggled his ass. My hand couldn't help but smack it, and he groaned in response, driving me to mark the other cheek as well. Since we'd engaged in the enlightened lifestyle Diamond and Easton lived, my guys and I had discovered new things not only about each other but ourselves as well. With Benny, he loved being spanked. Especially when there was a cock filling his ass, and as the owner of one of those cocks, I had to admit it felt damn good to be buried inside when his muscles would ripple and flex around you while the spanking took place.

I squirted a generous amount in my hand, running a finger through to warm it before applying it to his hole. Slipping in the first fingertip, reminded me how much I loved prepping him. The feel of my finger sliding in and out, watching it disappear. In and out. I got lost in this each and every time, usually to the tune of Benny finding his words and yelling at me to hurry the hell up and fuck him. But tonight, the three of us would be extra cautious, venturing into this new realm. With the second and third finger joining in, he began fucking himself in earnest on my digits, moaning with each push. River stroked both their cocks, watching the expressions on Benny's face and smiling up at him.

When I knew he was good and ready, I slathered River and I up. River laid there, hands behind his head, eyes closed with a blissed-out look on his face, "enjoying this Riv?" I teasingly asked, knowing I was enjoying this just as much as he was.

"You know I am, but if you keep this up I'm gonna come far too soon," he warned me.

"Got it," I said, feeling I was in much the same position. "You ready Benny?"

"More than," he tilted his head to the side, first kissing me before leaning over to do the same to River. I held River's cock upright for him to lower himself onto it, taking it in stride as his body adjusted to the progressive intrusion. Even though I was sitting back, watching Benny ride River. Even being a non-participant, I found this hot as fuck. I wanted to touch myself but knowing what was coming up already had me teetering on the edge, so I ignored that need.

"I'm ready," Benny announced, snapping me from my reverie. When he leaned forward, seeing the muscles at his entrance tightly gripping River's cock, I honestly didn't know how this was going to work.

I crawled up the bed, straddling River's legs up to where Benny sat. The pads of my thumbs massaged the muscles. I was blindly feeling for any gaps for which I could hope to enter through. This position was virginal to me and the fear creeping forward in my mind had me second-guessing the whole act. But when the muscles gave way, and my thumbs slipped inside, I had renewed hope.

"Hold on Benny," I told him, "I want to add more lube just in case." I hoped the additional lubricant would make it easier to slide in and reduce the pain I knew he was going to feel. I'm not sure I'm man enough to take on two cocks at one time, so I had to give Benny major kudos for his willingness even to attempt this.

My dick looked like porno prep gone wrong, and when I lined it up, it slid right out my hand. Every time I gripped it, my hand would slide off. *Shit*. Reality vs. porn, not only do you not get a plumber to show up at your house five minutes after you call him, but your moves don't always go off as smoothly as they do on the screen.

"Everything all right back there?" River called out to me.

"Um, yeah. Lube malfunction," I replied, lining up again. I more or less shoved the head in and due to the tightness surrounding it, it held. So much for making this a memorable event... "You okay Benny?"

"Yeah, push in a little bit more."

The tightness made it a challenge to get inside, I thought for sure I was gonna split Benny's ass wide open. If that happened, I'd never be the same again. But fuck me, the deeper I got, the tighter it became, and I damn near came every time I pushed.

"Hold up!" River shouted, "his face is intensely contorted."

"Fuck, Benny, want me to pull out?"

"No!" he screamed, "just...wait...please."

"It's like my dick is in a vise," I said aloud, really wishing I hadn't.

"If anyone moves, I'm blowing my load," River informed us, I had to laugh considering I felt the same way.

"Guys," Benny panted, "one of you is right up against my prostate so a couple quick moves, and it's over for me."

"Babe, we are right there with you," I informed him before gently kissing his shoulder.

"Okay, let me see if I can move now," he told us.

As Benny lifted, I gripped both mine and River's cocks firmly in hand so he'd come back down on them at the same time. I was surprised to see that worked out quite well. River took Benny's erection in hand and started jerking it. I knew we both need- ed him to come first before we'd allow ourselves to, kinda like some unwritten code we had, almost a courtesy so to speak. And if River was being affect- ed by the pressure like I was— he was ready to blow.

"Ah, ah. Gonna...Come!" Benny yelled, his channel pulsed around us as he rode out the waves and literally pulled the orgasm from me.

"Benny!" I yelled as I came.

At the same moment, River yelled, "Benny!"

Benny's worn out, sweat and paint-covered body collapsed on top of River, forcing us both out of him.

I picked him up, "River, can you get the shower started for us?" I asked as I carried Benny into the bathroom. With the water up to temp, I sat Benny down on the bench. River, and I proceeded to wash him, working in tandem as a team before taking care of our own needs. The entire scene made me think of the necessary aftercare Diamond had taught us about during our first time joining them in their dungeon. Seems that need extends far past a BDSM scene. Any lover worth their weight should always take care of their partners needs first.

We laid him down between us in bed, massaging his tired limbs, "Friday," he murmured.

"Friday for what love?" I asked.

"Friday for the courthouse."

River and I looked at each other, and the smile he gave me was full of love, not uncertainty, "Friday it is," River replied, agreeing with Benny before leaning over to kiss me. Today was Sunday, by the end of the week, I'd be a married man.

Poor Benny was the last of us to get out of bed the next morning, groaning and hissing with each step he took.

"Benny baby, why don't you sit down?" River asked him as he came into the kitchen. He and I were already clicking away on our laptops, cups of fresh coffee in hand.

"Sit," I told him, gesturing to his usual seat, "let me get your coffee." After I finished mixing it the way he liked, I snagged a croissant off the tray, setting both in front of him on the table. "Here you go," I said, kissing the top of his head before taking my seat. "I was doing some research, and we have to wait three days after we apply for the license before we can use it. I'm heading to the lawyers in a few minutes to meet with him about drawing up the paperwork for the three of us to sign. Do you guys have anything to add to it?"

"Well, not that I have much, but what I do have I'd like to have in writing that it goes to you and Benny if I were to die before either of you," River added.

"Same here. And may I point out how depressing our happy moment is becoming? Talk of death at the same time as a marriage. Ugh, why?" Benny protested, dropping his head into his hands.

"Unfortunately, guys, it seems you can't have one without the other anymore," I told them, draining the rest of my coffee. "I'm off to see the wizard,"

I announced, kissing them before heading out to meet with the lawyer.

The meeting with him was pretty uneventful, he seemed unmoved by my requests and told me to bring Benny and River in tomorrow to sign the documents before we headed over to get our license. On the way home, I stopped by Diamond's.

Diamond answered the door, clearly surprised to see me there, "Dude, what's up? You never stop by without calling first."

"Um, I have something I need to talk to you about. It's kind of important," I said, shifting nervously from foot to foot.

"I assumed so. Otherwise, you would've just texted it to me. Come on in, have a seat. You want something to drink?" He asked.

"Nah man, I'm good but thanks. I um," I trailed off. Fuck, why was this so hard? "So last night Benny, River and I were talking and we decided to get married."

He raised an eyebrow, questioningly, "How exactly does that work when that's illegal?"

"Well, the whole thing fell into place. I started talking about how I could make sure they were taken care of if something happened to me. Then I mentioned it would be easier if we were married then no one could fight them for anything. One thing led to another and River said I could marry Benny legally, make him the executor and then we could do a commitment ceremony later for the three of us and voila, it was decided. I just met with the band's lawyer, he's drawing up the documents, and Benny wants to go to the courthouse on Friday."

"Wow," he said, blowing out a breath, "that was one hell of a night you guys had."

"Yeah but I need to know that you're okay with it before we move forward with anything," I told him.

"Me?" he asked, more than confused, "how do I fit into this equation exactly?"

"I don't want you to feel like I'm stealing your thunder. You and Easton just got engaged and are planning your wedding, and I feel like we're kinda fucking that up for you."

"Ha-ha, Mickey, I would never in a million years think that. I'm happy for you guys, I really am. I've never seen you happier than you are when you're with them. Congrats," he said, pulling me into a hug and tugging on my hair, "what's this?" he handed me a chunk of something red. As soon as the scent hit my nose, I knew what it was.

My face flushed, "Oh, um. Strawberry body paint."

Again, he burst into laughter. That deep, hearty laugh that was genuinely Diamond. "You, my friend, have a little freaky-freak inside you."

I couldn't help but smile at that. "Thanks, I appreciate that. Ah, minus the freak comment but I was wondering if you'd be willing to stand up for me?

You know, be my best man. River is going to stand up for Benny, and I'd like my best friend to do the same for me."

"Dude, I'd be fucking honored," Diamond said before hugging me again.

CHAPTER SIX

Diamond

"East, guess what?" I called out after I shut the door when Mickey left.

He came running out of the office and into the foyer, "What's wrong?" he scanned the room, looking for something that wasn't there.

"What are you looking for?" I asked him, not sure if he was hearing voices or what the hell was up.

"What are you yelling about? Is someone here? Is something wrong?" he blurted out in a panic.

"Oh... ha, no. Sorry about that but Mickey was here, he just left. Nothing happened, well, not really."

"You mean to tell me I hung up on the caterer I've been trying to get a hold of for a week for no reason at all?" his voice escalated as he got to the end of that. *Oops.* Easton was not only overseeing the last-minute shit for the tour, but he was also planning our wedding for when we got back from Europe with Maiden. I'd asked multiple times to help, but he politely declined each request.

"Sorry I was just excited. Guess what?" I asked again.

"Okay, I give. What?" He asked, throwing his hands in the air in exasperation.

"Mickey and Benny are getting married!" I announced.

"Um, what? What about River? Have I entered some sort of alternate universe?" Yeah, I didn't handle this as well as I could've, and he was getting frustrated with me which I totally understood.

"Sorry, let me start from the beginning." I proceeded to share with him everything that Mickey had just told me, and by the end, he had a clear understanding. "Are you mad they're getting married before us?" I asked him when I'd finished explaining the situation.

"No, not at all and the fact that they decided to wait to hold their commitment ceremony until after our wedding says a lot to me. I more than understand Mickey's concern with making sure they're taken care of if anything were to happen to him. Especially considering we're heading back out on the road," he somberly added that last part and I knew we were both recalling the accident now.

I needed to change the subject and fast, choosing to switch to our impending nuptials, "Hey babe, how can I help you with the wedding stuff?" While I was afraid recounting those memories could set back the progress Easton made in his therapy, I also knew he was in his element by taking the proverbial bull by the horns and running with the wedding plans.

"There's nothing for you to do," he once again reiterated, kissing the tip of my nose which I found odd, yet I still smiled stupidly over it.

"We've got this honey," my mom told me as she walked into the room and snagged the invitations off the table, affixing postage stamps to them. I didn't even know where the wedding was going to be held. I told Easton to tell me where to be and when once he was ready to. I trusted him implicitly and wanted it to be the wedding of his dreams. All that mattered to me was that he was mine.

"Dude," Jay came walking in, tossing a basketball at me, "let's go shoot some hoops."

Jay and I walked down to the basketball courts at the clubhouse, leaving mom and Easton behind to play wedding planners. They both seemed kinda relieved to have us out of their hair. It was nice living in a gated community, rarely were we bothered by more than a couple of curious teens who usually ended up joining us for a game or two.

"So," Jay said, taking the first shot, "you sure about this whole marriage thing?" He dribbled, stepped back, and took a shot which I easily blocked.

"What exactly are you getting at?" I asked, faking to the right and landing a perfect two-pointer.

"The infamous womanizer Diamond Taylor, one and done now. No one else forever?"

"You've read the rags. You and the entire fucking world knows I've bagged my fair share of the female population. But yeah, for me this man is my one and done. My forever," I assured him, reflecting on the moment when I knew Easton was *it* for me.

"I'm just busting your balls, bro," he teased, stealing the ball from me and laughing. "I like Easton. He doesn't take any shit from you, and you seem happy."

"I am really fucking happy. I've got a great man, I've got my family back, and I've got a kick-ass job. What more could a man ask for?"

"True dat!" He yelled, fist-bumping me before taking a swig out of his water bottle.

"How are things with you and Nathan? He hasn't been around much lately," I asked as I took a seat beside him on the bench. I hoped things were good, Jay seemed happy whenever I'd see them together, but I still wasn't quite sure where the big brother boundaries were.

He sighed, "I think it's going pretty good. Neither one of us has done the relationship thing before, and he's still a little skittish."

"Understandable given his past. Give him time, but make sure he knows you're always there for him. Sometimes it's hard to do when you feel ignored, but that poor kid has a shit ton of demons to work through," I did my best to try and sound reassuring, but not so sure I'd succeeded given the defeated look that crossed his face. "Come on, let's head back and jump in the pool."

The walk back was quiet, not a word passed between us. When we got home, we found mom and Easton sharing a bottle of wine and giggling, which to me made everything right in my world. How was I so lucky to have won this man's heart? And to top it off, my mother and brother both adored him. They say sometimes you have to go to hell and back to appreciate what you have. My family and I, we had seen hell and lived under Satan's rule. It may have taken us some time to claw our way out of the realm of the damned, but when we reached the surface, it made the battle won more than worth it.

Later that night when we were lying in bed, I was flipping mindlessly through the cable channels, and Easton was reading Ann Lister's new Rock Gods East Coast Label book one, A Rhythm You Feel. She was his must-read author. He fanboyed over her and pre-ordered every one of her books, "East, do you think we need to know more about each other's past conquests?"

"Not unless you have random kids running around that you need to tell me about. What brought this on?" he asked, setting his iPad aside.

"There's not a literal chance in hell that any little drummers are running around. I'm no fool, I double wrapped my tool," I said, winking at him. He rolled his eyes and laughed. "I was thinking about that shit that went down with Joey and Stoli. I don't want there ever to be anything between us. I'm an open book with you. If you ever want to know anything, all you need to do is ask me."

"Babe, I was there many, many, many. Did I use enough many's? Times when you and your conquests," he finger-quoted the word *conquests*, "were engaging with each other, shall we say? So no, I'm good with the information I already have stored away. I am more than satisfied with what I already know about the man I fell in love with and will soon be marrying."

"Hey, what were you and my mom giggling about when Jay and I got home?"

He took his time answering, taking off his glasses, and setting them and his iPad on the nightstand before shutting off the light. Generally, he didn't take this long to answer me, so I wasn't sure what was swirling around inside that brilliant head of his.

"I think you need to talk to your mom about that. It shouldn't come from me."

"Um, what shouldn't come from you?" something about this was setting my hackles on end.

"Have you noticed my dad is coming around a lot more?" he asked me.

"Well yeah, but I know you guys are getting the last-minute shit for the trip hashed out. What's going on Easton? My mom's not going with us is she?" While I like having her around and she seemed to enjoy the awards show, I wasn't sure life on the road would work well for her. Or for me for that matter.

"Yes, we are, although I've pretty much got that all wrapped up. Your mom and my dad are...talking," he said, eyeing me curiously.

Talking...talking. Oh, ding, ding, ding, ding—light bulb! "What the fuck?"

"Calm down Diamond. They're both adults. They're both single, and they're just talking, which I think you need to do the same with her. Let her know it's okay to see other people. I know your dad hasn't been gone long, but I get the impression he checked out of their relationship a long time ago." That's my Easton, always the levelheaded one. As usual, he was right. Mom didn't need my approval, but I'm sure she'd like to hear it just the same.

I couldn't deny he wasn't right. My father treated my mother more like one of his minions than a wife. *But still...*

"Grr," I growled without meaning to. Seems a normal response for me most of the time.

After breakfast the following morning, my mom came over to help Easton with more wedding plans. "Morning, mom," I said, kissing her cheek. "Want some coffee?"

"Oh, that would be lovely. Thank you, Ethan," she sat her purse down, taking a seat at the kitchen table.

"Want something to eat?" I asked as I placed the steaming mug in front of her.

"No, thank you, I already ate."

"Hey mom, can we talk about something?" *Ugh, why was I struggling with this?*

"Sure, honey, what's up?"

"I um. Hey, you're a single woman out on the prowl now, and I was just ugh, um was wondering if anyone's caught your eye yet?" *Jesus Diamond, sound like a dumbass much?*

"Ethan, what are you getting at exactly?"

"I guess what I'm trying to say is it's okay if you want to date. I want you to be happy," *did that come out right? I am so not good at this...*

"Well, not that I'd need your approval if I were ready to date," her eyes bore into me, reminding me that I was the child and she was the parent. "Your father hasn't been gone very long, and I'm not sure what the proper protocol is for this," she said, staring down into her cup, reminding me of how Jay and I had found her in our childhood kitchen the day after dad had died.

I reached out, placing my hand atop hers, "Sorry mom, I didn't mean to overstep. I don't know what or even if there is a protocol for this sort of thing, but what I do know is that dad checked out on us long before he took his last breath. You deserve to be happy. Hell, we all deserve to be happy after what he put us through. So, in all honesty, I say fuck whatever protocol there is and enjoy what's left of our lives."

"Ethan!" she yelled, smacking my hand, "language son."

"Sorry mom, but you know what I mean," it's incredible how quickly a scolding from your mother reverts you to a childlike state of mind.

"I do son, and I appreciate it. This is just something I have to work through on my own. Right now, I'm enjoying spending time with my sons and planning your wedding with my future son-in-law. He really is fantastic, Ethan. I adore him." The depth of sincerity in her eyes spoke came out in her words.

"Thanks, mom, so do I."

"Is everything all right in here?" Easton asked us as he entered the kitchen.

"Yeah babe, it is," I stood, pulling him into my arms. "I'll be downstairs. If you need me, text and I'll come right up," I kissed him, leaving those two to their plans, beyond elated they got along as well as they did. Everything easily could've gone south given the way we were raised. I fully expected my mom to be as homophobic as my asshole father was. Thankfully there was still enough of her true self intact, even after the years of abuse she'd suffered.

Dead or not, thinking about that man always got me riled up. I stuffed my AirPods in, cranked up my metal madness workout playlist, and ran my ass off on the treadmill. Twenty minutes later, when that hadn't sated the funk, I beat the hell out of the punching bag until my fists were numb. Exhausted, my sweaty ass passed out on the sectional couch in the basement, which was where Easton found me sometime later.

"Hey D," he whispered in my ear, at the same time, I felt something cold on my arm and jumped.

"What the?" I said, spotting the bottle of water in his hands.

Laughing, he handed it to me, "I thought you might need this. Everything okay?"

I took a swig before pulling him onto my lap, needing to feel him close, grounding me. Dozing off to thoughts of my father didn't make for a peaceful slumber. "It is now that you're here."

"You sweet talker you," he brushed the hair stuck to my forehead off to the side, "now, tell me what's wrong."

"Ugh, I don't even know anymore. Every time I think I'm past the shit storm caused by the sperm donor, something pops back into my skull and sets me off again. This morning, I did as you suggested and talked to my mom. By the end of the conversation, I was pissed off at him all over again. I mean, what the fuck? He's not even alive, and yet he still gets under my skin."

"Babe, look at me," when I didn't move my head, he did it for me. "There are some demons we never get past, some that go away on their own and some we need assistance with getting past. Your dad may be the latter of the three for you. It takes a strong man to admit something is wrong, but it takes an even stronger man to seek the help he needs to fix it. You helped me in my time of need, let me help you during yours."

I knew what he was getting at, but I wasn't ready to take that step. Call it pride, call it stupidity. Call it whatever the fuck you wanted, but outside of

Easton I wasn't prepared to talk to another living soul about my daddy issues.

"I know that look all too well. You know I'm here for you, no matter what you need. Now let's get you cleaned up. The moms are taking over our kitchen to cook dinner for our band family since we're leaving this weekend."

He did his best to pull me up, and I had to give him props for trying, so I let him win. This time...

CHAPTER SEVEN

Easton

Sitting in the dining room, glancing at the happy faces of our massive family, and enjoying a meal together in our home, one word came to mind.

Complete...

That was how my life felt.

Family...

I'd had it since birth. Blood wise that is but now I had it tenfold.

Family doesn't need blood to form a bond, it only needs to have a heart.

No truer words have been written. No truer words have been spoken, and now I finally understood the meaning behind these infamous words the Social Sinners band members lived by. The band who'd become my family, welcoming me in like they had so many others. Arms wide open into their judgment-free zone. They never saw me as I had. The geeky wallflower no one paid attention to, his face forever buried in his electronic forms of communication. I was Easton to them. Leader, friend, lover...*family.*

Never in my wildest dreams did I imagine I not only had a chance for more than a one-night stand with the notorious bad boy, Diamond Taylor, whom I'd pined after for as long as I could remember. But that I'd be marrying him and spending the rest of my life in his arms. *My forever.*

I'd do anything for him, and the way he stood by me during my dark times, through rehab and even stuck around afterward more than showed me he'd do the same for me. No questions asked... he loved me more than I ever thought possible.

On Friday we'd bear witness to another brother saying I do before embarking upon the biggest tour in the history of our band. Being a part of this, watching these guys grow brought tears to my eyes. When I first accepted this job fresh out of college, that was precisely what I thought of it— it was just a job, a way to get my feet wet and prove to my father that I could follow in his footsteps. Neither of us expected it to turn into so much more than that. And yet, here we were, breaking bread as a family with them.

Across the room, I watched my father smile as he chats with Sharon and the other parents, each time he turns her way, his face lights up. I'm not sure she notices, although the blush she wears could be interpreted as otherwise. Honestly, I can't remember the last time my father wore a genuine smile. My mother was slowly draining the life from him over the years. How he lived in a loveless relationship for as long as he did, I'll never know.

When we return from the tour, Joey and Stoli would be embarking on a songwriting collaboration with none other than the infamous frontman of his favorite band, Korn's Jonathan Davis. The very man Joey idolized. And to help orchestrate that collaboration filled me to the brim with pride. These were my boys, my team, my brothers, and when they were happy, so was I.

So much happened over the years with surprises hid around each corner. Some were good, some were bad, but each time we rode the waves together, we surfaced victoriously.

Wanna talk about being thrown for a loop? How about an impromptu meeting with your boyfriends' mother on the wake of his father's death? The drive over to her house felt like I was walking the plank, but once she realized being gay wasn't the plague her husband preached about, it opened the gates for us to form a bond. One that I was more than grateful for.

Planning our wedding with her has been a dream. My mother had no interest, hell, if I mentioned it to her she'd only say it was a waste of her time and proceed to try and get into Diamond's pants, and neither of us wanted to deal with the hot mess that she'd become. Working with Sharon, mom as she'd asked me to call her, completed the family circle for me.

They say hindsight is always twenty-twenty, and looking back I find that statement to be more than true. All the years my mother ignored me in favor of living her own life, I never paid much attention to her because my father was always there for me. He's the one I went to the Mariners games with, the one who came to my school functions and the one who took me under his wing to learn every inch of the family business that I could. He was my true parent and mentor, always telling me he's proud of me and never questioning my decisions. Sure, I made a bad one from time to time, but the first words out of his mouth with each was, '*Easton, how do you suggest we go about fixing this?*' There was never words of condemnation, always taught to chalk it up to a lesson learned and that everything was fixable. I couldn't have asked for a better cheerleader to be in my corner.

It was important to me that our wedding be memorable for both Diamond and me. And planning it with Sharon was amazing. The Ides of March at Thornewood Castle in Lakewood, Washington, will be where we say I do. We've rented the entire venue, coming in the night before and leaving the night after so no one is rushed to go home afterward. Due to the time of year we've chosen, the wedding will be held indoors in their great hall. March in Seattle is exceptionally wet, making an outdoor wedding impossible. We'll be walking down the aisle, hand in hand to the song Diamond wrote for me, Character Flaws, the same song I proposed to him while Joey and Stoli performed it. No words will be sung this time though; only the music will be playing in the background. I did, however, opt for matching tuxedos, or monkey suits as my lovely fiancé likes to call them. Something I know he'll growl at but will ultimately wear because he knows how much it means to me.

We kept the guest list to a comfortable number. We're only inviting family, immediate friends, and of course our extended family, Maiden Voyage. It's an all-inclusive weekend for those joining us, and I have another surprise in store for Diamond, one that was quite fitting given who I was marrying. Joe senior was getting ordained so he could marry us, at his request. He became a father to Diamond when he was cast aside by his own, and I knew how much it would mean to him to see Joe do this for us.

Mickey is going to be Diamond's best man, as Diamond is doing for him this coming Friday. For me, having no siblings, and since I was marrying my best friend, I asked my dad to stand up for me. He got teary-eyed when I made the request and embraced me so quickly that he knocked the wind out of me.

My life was full, filled with love as was our home at this very moment. Each hug given as our friends and family filed out, calling it a night was genuine. No forced, fake feelings. Only real ones. The kind you knew wouldn't stab you in the back as you walked away.

Due to the stature of our persona, dad suggested Mickey make an appointment for Friday with a friend of his who's a judge in his chambers for their nuptials, to avoid the public eye. I asked Fizzbo from Ventura Security to send us a couple hired hands just in case because more than likely someone would spot us and leak the news before we even left the building.

"So," Diamond threw his arm around my shoulder after we'd locked the door behind our last guest, "Any chance you're gonna tell me when or where we're tying the knot?"

"Absolutely, I was waiting for you to ask. Up until now, you only said to let you know when the time came. The date is the Ides of March, and the place is Thornewood Castle in Lakewood."

"Hmm, somewhat ominous," he added.

"Well, you have internet available to you so Google it," I winked.

"Do I have to wear a monkey suit?"

"You know it," I replied.

"Where's my prize for that?"

"Waiting downstairs," I replied, taking off at a run and almost made it to the landing before his hands snaked around my waist and lifted me in the air. I loved it when he took control. I was always on duty, in control of our daily business lives, knee-deep in wedding plans. Don't get me wrong, I'm not complaining but not to have to worry about decisions in the bedroom– or dungeon, in this case, was a huge relief. The one place I could shut my brain down and just...feel. I trusted Diamond without question, to take care of my needs.

With the door closed behind us, I disrobed, hanging my clothes on the hooks and awaited further instruction.

"What would you like tonight, my pet?" he asked, surprising me. Usually, he already knew what he wanted before we got down here.

"Nipple clamps, and a vibrating butt plug while Master serves ten lashes with my favorite flogger before fucking me," I told him, without pause.

"Seems my pet's put some thought into this. On the bed, face down, arms and legs spread out," Diamond ordered, and I shivered. As I took my place atop the bed, he retrieved the toys I'd requested. After he secured my wrists and ankles to the bedposts, he stripped and knelt between my legs. "I love you, my pet," he said as he always did before we assumed our roles.

"I love you too, Master," words spoken from my heart.

He reached around the front of me, pinching my nipples, pebbling them before attaching the clamps, I hissed when the teeth on the clamp bit into my flesh, a pain I enjoyed.

"Do you like that, my Pet?" he asked me.

"Very much, Master."

I heard him lube the plug before I felt his finger trace the outline of my entrance with the gelled substance, gliding in and out. I loved how it felt when he did that, and I could feel my body pull him inside as the muscles contracted around his fingers. He stared at it for a few minutes as his fingers stretched me before teasing my entrance with the plug. I could enjoy this for hours. I loved how it felt when my muscles expanded and contracted. Being fucked by a toy, his fingers, his cock– I found so much pleasure in everything he did to me. My ass was his to do with as he pleased. *Damn, I'm a lucky man.*

Once the plug was inserted, he sat back, admiring his handy work before clicking the toy on. One, two, on the third click I knew it was as high at it would go and it was pegging my spot relentlessly.

"God, you're beautiful," he whispered, and I whimpered. "I believe my pet requested ten strikes, correct?"

"Yes, Master."

"Count with me, please. One," he made the first strike, and I repeated after him. "Two," he struck the other cheek as I again counted with him. With each blow, he rotated cheeks until we reached ten.

"Is it my cock you wish to feel inside you now, my pet?" he asked, already knowing the answer but I knew he loved hearing it come from my lips.

"Please, Master," I plead, breathlessly waiting to feel the familiar fullness I associated with our love-making.

He pulled the plug out, making the final click to turn it off before tossing it aside. In one push, he plunged inside me, "My pet, the things you do to me. The way you make me feel," he growled, grabbing a fistful of my hair as he pounded my ass in earnest, giving me the fucking I craved. With each thrust, my balls painfully tightened as the pulsing at the base of my spine increased. "Tonight, I'm going to come before you. I'm going to fuck you until you scream and then I'm going to suck you dry until you're reduced to a panting, babbling mess," his words both excited and shocked me. "Do not come until you're in my mouth. Understood?"

"Ungh, yes...Master," my words were barely audible.

With both his hands now wound through my hair, he continued to pummel my ass until the pain I felt by holding off my release became unbearable.

"Fuck, I'm coming!" he yelled, filling me until he had nothing left to give. Quickly he released my restraints and flipped me over. My dick had leaked on the sheets, and I knew I was gonna blow as soon as he had me in his mouth. "Fuck my mouth," he ordered me, leaning over, and taking me inside his mouth.

I didn't think twice before gripping his hair so tightly I knew it had to be painful. I fucked his mouth with such intensity, hitting the back of his throat and making him gag. But I knew it wouldn't be for long. At last, I screamed at the top of my lungs as my warm release slid down his throat. I loved this ease between us for which we worked as one — more than anything I loved this man who made me...whole.

When we were done, he picked me up and carried me over to the couches, handing me a water bottle before covering us up while we came back down from our euphoric high. We dozed off for a bit before finally making our way upstairs, showering and slipping into a deep, peaceful sleep.

The rest of the week went by in a blur of last-minute details. Making sure the band's equipment was safely shipped off to meet us in Paris, packing our clothes and on Friday, meeting Mickey, Benny, and River at the judge's chambers. They asked that he keep it simple, for which he did. He made sure he held both his guy's hands in his, and as they said I do, he kissed River first and then Benny. It was important to him that River knew he held the same place in his heart as Benny did.

Bright and early Saturday morning, we boarded the Maiden Voyage jet at the executive terminal at SeaTac airport. First stop, JFK in New York to fuel and then onward to Paris for the first show of our tour.

SPECIAL ANNOUNCEMENT

I'm excited to announce a new series coming in 2020!
You'll finally get to know these fabulous guys who've been there for the Social Sinners crew throughout their journey as they kick off their double headlining European tour. Maiden Voyage will be a four-book series that dives into the lives of their guitarist Ryder Hampton, lead singer– Derek Masters, bass player– Jaxson Mathias and their drummer Alejandro "Shadow" Salazar.
But you know what's even better than that? Kicking off book 1, Ryder's Guardian will be a co-authored project with award-winning author, Ann Lister!

It's an absolute dream (fangirl down) for me to work with her. I've idolized Ann's work for as long as I can remember and I'm ecstatic to be collaborating with her.

So without further ado, I give you the cover for book 1– Ryder's Guardian:

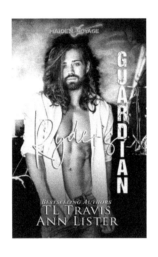

About the Author

TL Travis is an award-winning published author of LGBTQIA+ contemporary and paranormal romance and erotic musings that have earned "Best-Selling Author" flags in the US as well as Internationally.

By day she and her team of mild-mannered maintenance techs are ridding the world of those pesky broken things. In her free time, TL enjoys catching up with her family, attending concerts, wine tasting, and traveling.

Ann Lister's literary library:

OTHER BOOKS BY ANN LISTER

Looking At Forever
Smarturl.it/ALRG4
Erotic, MM, Rockstar, Romance
Book 5:
Meant For Me
Smarturl.it/ALRG5
Erotic, MM, Rockstar, Romance
Book 6:
Fighting His Fire
Smarturl.it/ALRG6
Erotic, MM, Rockstar, Romance
Book 7:
Beyond The Music
Smarturl.it/ALRG7
Erotic, MM, Rockstar, Romance
Book 8:
Forever At Sunrise
Smarturl.lit/ALRG8
Erotic, MM, Rockstar, Romance
Book 9:
Reinventing Us
Smarturl.it/ALRG9
Erotic, MFM, MM, Rockstar, Romance
__Guarding The Gods:__
Book 1:
Zac's Mulligan
Smarturl.it/ALGTG1
Erotic, MM, Romance
Book 2:

Honor And Pride
Smarturl.it/ALGTG2
Erotic, MM, Romance
Book 3:
More Than My Words
Smarturl.it/ALGTG3
Erotic, MM, Romance
Book 4:
The Black Key Journal
Smarturl.it/ALGTG4
Erotic, MM, Romance
Band Of Brothers:
Book 1:
For All The Right Reasons
Smarturl.it/ALBOB1
Erotic, Rockstar, Contemporary, Romance
Book 2:
Beat Of His Own Drums
Smarturl.it/ALBOB2
Erotic, MM, Rockstar, Contemporary, Romance
The Illicit Heat Series:
Book 1:
Model Student
Smarturl.it/ALEH1
Erotic, MM, Romance
Book 2:
Climbing The Longhorn
Smarturl.it/ALEH2
Erotic, MM, Romance

Book 3:
Billionaire's Toy
Smarturl.it/ALEH3
Erotic, MM, Romance
EH4:
Snowballs For My Valentine
Smarturl.it/ALSnowballs
Erotic, MM, Romance
__Stand-alones:__
Sheet Music
Smarturl.it/ALSheetMusic
Erotic , MF, Rockstar, Contemporary, Romance
Covered in Lace
Smarturl.it/ALLacey
Erotic, MF, Rockstar, Romance
Without a Doubt
Smarturl.it/ALWAD
Erotic, MF, Contemporary, Romance
An Early Spring
Smarturl.it/ALSpring
Erotic, Contemporary, Romance
Moved By You
Smarturl.it/ALMovedByYou
Erotic, MM, Romance

Milton Keynes UK
Ingram Content Group UK Ltd.
UKHW040854110923
428455UK00001B/14